CLEVER CUB
Learns to Share

Bob Hartman
Illustrated by Steve Brown

DAVID C COOK
transforming lives together

CLEVER CUB LEARNS TO SHARE
Published by David C Cook
4050 Lee Vance Drive
Colorado Springs, CO 80918 U.S.A.

Integrity Music Limited, a Division of David C Cook
Brighton, East Sussex BN1 2RE, England

The graphic circle C logo is a registered trademark of David C Cook.

All rights reserved. Except for brief excerpts for review purposes,
no part of this book may be reproduced or used in any form
without written permission from the publisher.

All Scripture paraphrases are based on the ESV® Bible (The Holy Bible, English
Standard Version®), copyright © 2001 by Crossway, a publishing ministry of
Good News Publishers. Used by permission. All rights reserved.

Library of Congress Control Number 20211949485
ISBN 978-0-8307-8255-0

© 2022 Bob Hartman
Illustrations by Steve Brown. Copyright © 2022 David C Cook

The Team: Laura Derico, Stephanie Bennett, Judy Gillispie, James Hershberger, Susan Murdock
Cover Design: James Hershberger
Cover Art: Steve Brown

Printed in China
First Edition 2022

1 2 3 4 5 6 7 8 9 10

011222

Clever Cub was **ANGRY**.

The little bear **STOMPED** into the cave.

"What's wrong, son?" Papa Bear asked. He was just getting ready to go fishing.

"Skippy Squirrel!" Clever Cub grumbled. "He won't play with me anymore!"

"Hmm. You didn't growl at him again, did you?" Papa Bear chuckled, remembering the last time Skippy had run off.

"Because he might drop it! Or lose it! Or **BREAK** it!" Clever Cub stomped as he talked. "And it is the best and **BIGGEST** pinecone I ever found!"

"Ohhh, I guess Skippy often drops or loses or breaks things, right?" Papa Bear asked.

"Well … no," Clever Cub said. "But he *might*!"

"So you just didn't want to share?" Papa Bear said. "Is that it?"

"Maybe," Clever Cub muttered.

"Hmm. That *is* a problem." Papa Bear thought for a minute. "You know, I remember a Bible story that might help. I know you **LOVE** Bible stories."

Clever Cub cheered up. "Were there pinecones in the Bible?"

"I don't know. Maybe. But there were *definitely* fish," Papa Bear said.

"I **LOVE** fish!" Clever Cub shouted. "Like those slippery salmon you catch!"

Papa Bear started telling the story as he waded into the stream. "This story is about a boy with some fish and bread."

"I like fish and *more fish* better," Clever Cub said.

Papa Bear agreed. "Yes, me too. But this boy brought his fish and bread up on a hill where more than **FIVE THOUSAND** people had gathered."

"What were they all doing there?" Clever Cub asked.

"Following Jesus," Papa Bear answered. "The people came a lo-o-ong way to see and hear Jesus. And everyone was HUNGRY."

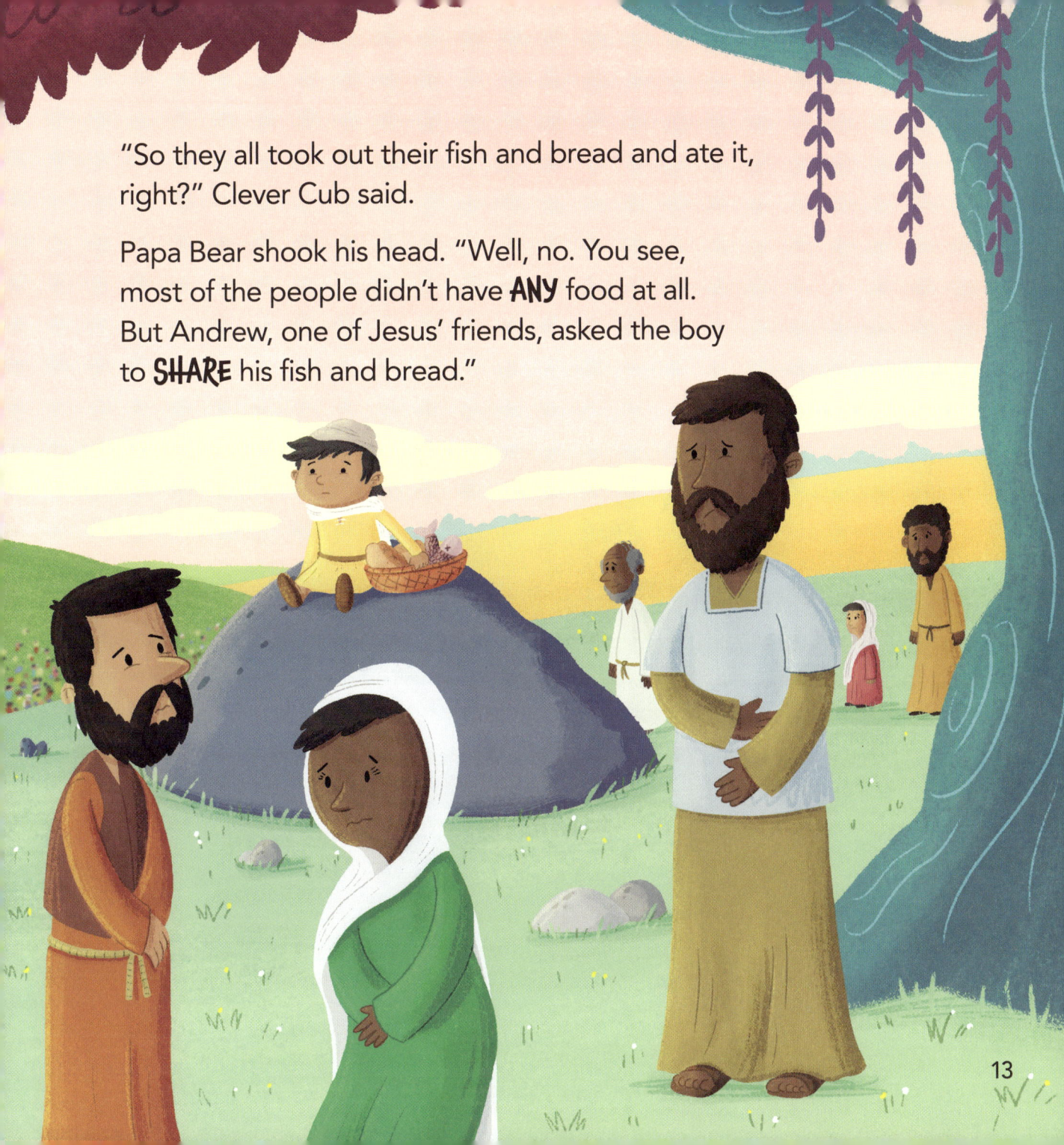

"So they all took out their fish and bread and ate it, right?" Clever Cub said.

Papa Bear shook his head. "Well, no. You see, most of the people didn't have **ANY** food at all. But Andrew, one of Jesus' friends, asked the boy to **SHARE** his fish and bread."

"*Share?* With *five thousand* people?!"
Clever Cub looked amazed.
"Did he have a HUGE picnic basket?"

"No," Papa Bear said.
"He had only two fish and five loaves of bread.
But he was willing to share what he had.
So he gave the food to Andrew.
And Andrew gave it to Jesus."

Clever Cub scratched his nose and thought hard.
"Did Jesus **EAT** the boy's lunch?"

"No!" Papa Bear said. "Jesus **PRAYED** and thanked God for the food. Then He broke the fish and bread into pieces and gave them to His friends to pass out to the crowd."

"Those must have been really **TINY** pieces!" Clever Cub said.

"That's the amazing thing," Papa Bear said. "They weren't tiny at all. Everyone ate and ate and **ATE** until they were full. In fact, there were 12 baskets of leftovers!"

"**WOW**!" shouted Clever Cub.

"So, how do you think the people felt then?" Papa Bear asked.

"HAPPY!" Clever Cub said.

"And how about Jesus?"

"Happy too." Clever Cub smiled.

"And what about the boy who shared?" Papa Bear asked.

Clever Cub scratched his nose. He always did that when he was thinking. "I guess he was happy too."

Then Papa Bear said, "So, what about **YOU**? Do you think you can share with Skippy?"

"Hmm. Skippy **HATES** fish!" Clever Cub pulled on his ear. He always did that when he was a little confused. Then he said quietly, "But he *does* like pinecones."

"I think if you share your pinecone, Skippy will be really happy," Papa Bear said. "And I will be happy and proud of you for sharing. But how will **YOU** feel?"

Clever Cub smiled. "Well, Skippy will probably want to play with me again. And that will make me really HAPPY."

"How happy?" Papa Bear asked.

Clever Cub thought for several moments. Finally, he answered. "As happy as a hungry bear with 12 baskets full of fish!"

For Clever Readers

Clever Cub is a curious little bear who **LOVES** to cuddle up with the Bible and learn about God! In this story, Clever Cub hears about a boy who shared his food, even though he had very little to give. You can read more about this miracle of Jesus in John 6:1–14. Clever Cub learns that sharing might not be so bad after all!

What's your favorite toy? Do you like to share it? Sometimes sharing is hard, but God helps us learn to give to others. He shares so much with us!
What can you share?